I'D RATHER STAY HOME

Authors

Carol Barkin
Elizabeth James

Photographer

Heinz Kluetmeier

 **RAINTREE EDITIONS**

Library of Congress Number: 75-19481

Published by  **RAINTREE EDITIONS**

A Division of
Advanced Learning Concepts, Inc.
Milwaukee, Wisconsin 53203

Distributed by   Childrens Press

1224 West Van Buren Street
Chicago, Illinois 60607

Library of Congress Cataloging in Publication Data

Barkin, Carol.
  I'd rather stay home.

  SUMMARY: Explores the fears and anxieties connected
with leaving home and starting school.
    1. Emotions—Juvenile literature.   2. Home and
school—Juvenile literature.   3. Fear—Juvenile
literature. [1. Emotions.   2. School] I. James,
Elizabeth, joint author.   II. Kluetmeier, Heinz.
III. Title.
BF723.E6B3   158'.24   75-19481
ISBN 0-8172-0030-4

I wish today wasn't the first day of school.

I'd like to stay home and play with my trucks

and airplanes.

Everybody says school will be lots of fun.

But I don't want to go.

My brother tells me about the playground at school.

He says, "You can hang by your knees on the rings."

My sister says, "Ms. Kimball tells funny stories.

And she might let you bring your pet snake

to school!"

I don't know. Maybe it will be okay.

But I don't know how to hang by my knees.

What if everyone else knows how to do things

I can't do?

Mom takes me to school on her way to work.

"I'll pick you up when school is over,"

she says.

"I bet you'll make a lot of new friends today."

But what if no one wants to play with me?

Ms. Kimball is waiting at the door when we

get to school.

"Hi, Jimmy. I'm glad to see you."

Ms. Kimball shows me where to hang my jacket.

"Come and meet some new friends, Jimmy,"

she says.

All the other kids seem to know

each other already.

Mom says goodbye.

"I have to go or I'll be late.

Have fun! I'll see you later."

Ms. Kimball smiles at me and takes my hand.

"Do you want to help Tom and Sarah build

with blocks?"

I tell her, "No!"

I sit down at a table piled with books.

16

Lots of kids are playing games.

No one asks me to play.

I wish it was time to go home.

What if Mom forgets to come back?

Sarah and Tom are building something.

It looks like a tunnel.

Sarah tells Tom, "We need big blocks

for the top."

I'd like to crawl through that tunnel.

Tom brings a big block from the corner, while

Sarah goes to get another block.

Tom can't put the block on the tunnel by himself.

Maybe I can help him.

Tom and Sarah and I finish building the tunnel.

We take turns crawling through it.

It's fun!

All of a sudden Tom asks me, "Hey, what's

your name?"

Ms. Kimball calls us to sit down with her.

She tells us a funny story about an elephant.

Tom and I can't stop laughing.

When Tom tries to say "elephant" and gets

mixed up, I start laughing all over again.

After rest time we play Farmer in the Dell.

I get to be the Farmer!

In the middle of the game the door opens.

It's Mom!

Is it time to go home already?

Ms. Kimball helps us put on our jackets.

Tom says, "See you tomorrow, Jimmy!"

"Okay!"

When we get home I ask Mom, "Can Tom come to

our house tomorrow after school?"

Design Interface Design Group